A NOTE TO PARE

Reading Aloud with Your Child

Research shows that reading books most valuable support parents car children learn to read.

- Be a ham! The more enthusiasm you display, the more your child will enjoy the book.
- Run your finger underneath the words as you read to signal that the print carries the story.
- Leave time for examining the illustrations more closely; encourage your child to find things in the pictures.
- Invite your youngster to join in whenever there's a repeated phrase in the text.
- Link up events in the book with similar events in your child's life.
- If your child asks a question, stop and answer it. The book can be a means to learning more about your child's thoughts.

Listening to Your Child Read Aloud

The support of your attention and praise is absolutely crucial to your child's continuing efforts to learn to read.

- If your child is learning to read and asks for a word, give it immediately so that the meaning of the story is not interrupted. DO NOT ask your child to sound out the word.
- On the other hand, if your child initiates the act of sounding out, don't intervene.
- If your child is reading along and makes what is called a miscue, listen for the sense of the miscue. If the word "road" is substituted for the word "street," for instance, no meaning is lost. Don't stop the reading for a correction.
- If the miscue makes no sense (for example, "horse" for "house"), ask your child to reread the sentence because you're not sure you understand what's just been read.
- Above all else, enjoy your child's growing command of print and make sure you give lots of praise. *You are your child's first teacher — and the most important one. Praise from you is critical for further risk-taking and learning.*

— Priscilla Lynch
Ph.D. New York University
Educational Consultant

Text and illustrations copyright © 1997 by David McPhail.
All rights reserved. Published by Scholastic Inc.
HELLO READER! and CARTWHEEL BOOKS and associated logos
are trademarks and/or registered trademarks of Scholastic Inc.

Library of Congress Cataloging-in-Publication Data

McPhail, David M.
    The great race/ by David McPhail.
        p.   cm. — (Hello reader! Level 2)
    Summary: To relieve their boredom, six barnyard friends decide to
hold a race.
    ISBN 0-590-84909-3
    [1. Domestic animals — Fiction. 2. Racing — Fiction.] I. Title.
    II. Series.
PZ7.M2427Grj   1997
[E]—dc21
                                                             97-2244
                                                             CIP
                                                             AC

10 9   0/0 01 02

Printed in the U.S.A.   24
First printing, December 1997

The Great Race

by David McPhail

Hello Reader! — Level 2

SCHOLASTIC INC.
Cartwheel ·B·O·O·K·S· ®
New York Toronto London Auckland Sydney

All of the barnyard animals were bored.

"Let's have a race," said the cow.
"Where?" asked the duck.

"Let's race around the world,"
said the goose.
"That's too far,"
said the rooster.

"Around the barnyard,"
said the pig.

The animals lined up
at the barnyard gate.
"When do we start?"
asked the duck.
"When I say go,"
said the dog.

The rooster started to run.
"You said go," he called,
"so I'm going!"

The other animals ran after him.
First the duck, then the goose,
the cow, and the dog.
The pig was last.

But the pig tripped and fell.
He rolled downhill . . .

past the goose, the duck,
the cow, and the dog.

He rolled right on top
of the rooster.
"Ooofff!" said the rooster.

The other animals stopped
to see if anyone was hurt.

"I'm fine," said the rooster.

"I'm dizzy," said the pig.

The race continued.

As the rooster ran past the henhouse,
the hens cheered loudly.

But he slipped in the mud.
So did everybody else.

All but the pig.

He was used to running
in the mud.

The pig passed the other animals.
The race was almost over.

"Puff, puff, puff,"
went the pig.

"Clomp, clomp, clomp,"
went the cow.

"Pant, pant, pant,"
went the dog.

The duck, the goose, and
the rooster used their wings
to go faster.
"Flap, flap, flap."

And the animals reached
the gate at the very same time.

"I won!" cried the duck.

"Me, too!" said the goose.

"So did I!" said the cow.

The rooster bowed.
"I'm the greatest!"

"I'm top dog,"
said the dog.

"I'm a champ,"
said the pig.

And they all were very happy
as they walked off to rest.